This book belongs to:

....

....

For Ruby—A.H. Benjamin

Editor: Alexandra Koken
Designer: Plum Pudding Design

Copyright © QEB Publishing 2012

First published in the United States by
QEB Publishing
3 Wrigley, Suite A
Irvine, CA 92618

www.qed-publishing.co.uk

A CIP record for this book is available from the Library of Congress.

ISBN 978 1 60992 233 7

Printed in China

Hens Don't Crow!

A.H. Benjamin

Illustrated by Rebecca Elliott

QEB Publishing

Rooster had a sore throat.
"Oh, no," he croaked.
"Who will wake up the farm
in the morning?"

"I will!" clucked Hen.
"How?" said Rooster.
"Hens don't crow!"

"Leave it to me," said Hen.

Hen found Cat sunning herself
by the barn doors.

"Listen," said Hen.
"Rooster is not feeling well.
So I'll be waking up the farm
tomorrow morning..."

"What?" meowed Cat. "Hens don't crow!"
"Never mind that," said Hen. "Just go tell the others."

Cat ran off to tell Dog.
She found him outside of his kennel.

"You won't believe this," said Cat.
"Hen is waking us up in the morning!"

"But she's a hen!" barked Dog.
"Hens don't crow!"

"I know," said Cat.
"You'd better spread
the word."

Dog scampered away. He found Pig in his sty.

"Guess what?" said Dog.
"Hen is waking us up in the morning!"

"Impossible," grunted Pig. "Hens don't crow!"
"Of course not," said Dog. "Go tell the others."

Pig trotted off in a hurry.
He found Cow under the old tree.

"Have you heard?" cried Pig.
"Hen is waking us up in the morning!"

"Nonsense!" mooed Cow.
"Everyone knows
hens don't crow!"

"Well, I never heard one," said Pig.
"I will go tell Horse," said Cow.
Horse was the oldest and wisest
animal on the farm.

Cow found Horse in his paddock.

"Hogwash!" he neighed when Cow told him the news.
"Hens don't crow!"

"That's what everyone
is saying," shrugged Cow.

"I will have a
word with that silly hen,"
said Horse.
"Where is she?"

But no one could find Hen.
"What are we going to do?" everyone cried.
"We can't rely on Hen.
We'll never get up in the morning!"

Hen watched
the hullabaloo from her
secret hiding place.

The animals were so worried
that they couldn't sleep.
So they all found ways to
pass the time...

Cat chased mice
in the barn.

Dog buried all of
his favorite bones.

Pig built an
enormous
mud castle.

Cow counted
stars in
the sky.

Horse neighed
his favorite tune.

Dawn came at last...

All of the animals
gathered in the farmyard.
Finally, Hen arrived.

"Good morning, everyone!" she said.
"Come on," they all said. "Let's hear you crow!"
"There's no need," laughed Hen. "You're all up!"

The animals stared at one another.
Of course they were—they hadn't gone to sleep!
How could they when they were so worried?

"You tricked us!
We thought
you were going
to crow!"

"Don't be silly," Hen said.
"Hens don't crow!"

Next Steps

Show the children the cover again. Could they have guessed what the story is about by looking at the cover?

Ask the children if they have ever visited a farm. What kind of animals did they see there? Do they know what the animals do on a farm? For instance a cow gives milk, a hen lays eggs, and so on.

Find out whether the children can recognize animals by the noises they make. Can they make the noise of a particular animal? A rooster, perhaps? Or a pig?

Try acting out the story together. There are plenty of different characters, and all of them are familiar to children. It will be noisy but fun!

Discuss the story with the children. The main theme is that it's wrong to underestimate people. We are all different, but we are all good at something.

In this story no one believed that Hen could wake up the farm, just because she can't crow. But she used her brain and did it her own way! Ask the children if they have ever found a new way of doing something or an unusual way of solving a problem.

Finally, see how many children would like to work on a farm for a day or two. Perhaps some of them would like to be farmers when they grow up. Do they know what's involved? Talk about various farm jobs.